CHARLES the LION DOG

Written by Joseph C. Daniel

Illustrated by Pamela S. Barcita

STORYARTSMEDIA

CHARLES THE LION DOG
Text Copyright © 2013 Joseph C. Daniel
Illustrations Copyright © 2013 Pamela S. Barcita
All rights reserved.

No part of this book may be reproduced or transmitted in any form or by any means,
electronic or mechanical, including photocopying, recording, or by any information storage
and retrieval system, without written permission from the publisher.

Published by Story Arts Media
PO Box 1230, Boulder, CO 80306
www.storyartsmedia.com

ISBN: 978-0-9889754-9-1 (hardcover)
Library of Congress Control Number: 2013952198

www.charlestheliondogbook.com

Cover and Interior Design by Barcita & Barcita and Joseph E. Daniel

Special thanks to Gail Stenberg; Samantha Atkinson; Caden & Kinley Shannon;
Luisa, John & Skipper; Ken, Robin & the B Boys; youth readers Noah Asher Boone,
Caroline Holleman Smith, Reagan Willin Heller & Elizabeth Mandilyn Chrisman;
and all of our generous backers on Kickstarter for their support.

CHARLES THE LION DOG has been produced and printed in a manner compliant with the
Consumer Product Safety Improvement Act (CPSIA) which protects children from products
containing unsafe levels of lead and phthalates. Printed in the United States
October 2013 at Bookmasters in Ashland, Ohio. Job #50000225

Dedicated to Daniel Painter, whose imaginative mind and
fun-loving personality created the *real* Lion Dog. As Charles' owner
in real life, he understood the broad appeal a Lion Dog would have for children
all over the world. In one sense, young Daniel's love for his dog in this story
is a reflection of the love the real Daniel has for the real Charles.

Scan code for video.

THIS BOOK BELONGS TO

_____

On the morning of his eighth birthday Daniel woke up with one thing on his mind – lions! Now this wasn't a particularly odd thing. Daniel was crazy about lions. He had seen them at the zoo, and they were his favorite animal. Lions were so big and so strong and could roar very loudly. Daniel really liked them. When he learned to read he read many books about lions, and he had many pictures of lions on his bedroom wall. He was always thinking about lions.

That same morning a big dog awoke in a cage at the animal shelter. He had been found about three weeks ago lost in the city. He had no collar or tags, and his hair was very long and thick. The people at the shelter took him in, named him Charles and liked him very much. They thought that such a nice dog must have belonged to someone who had loved him very much. They cleaned him up as best they could with all that hair, and hoped that his owner would soon visit the shelter while out searching to find him.

When no one came to claim Charles he was put up for adoption. Several people looked at him but decided he was too big and furry to be a good pet. Charles was lonely at the shelter and just wanted to go home with one of the friendly people who peered into his cage.

Back at Daniel's house his parents had just told him that on his birthday he would be old enough to have a pet of his own and they wanted to know what he might like. "I want a lion," Daniel had answered excitedly. His mother had smiled, then said, "That might be a bit hard to arrange, Daniel. A lion is a wild animal and very big. It would be a problem in a house. And it would cost a lot of money just to feed it. Maybe another kind of pet would be better, like a puppy or how about a kitten?" She suggested that when a kitten grew up to be a cat, Daniel could pretend it was a miniature lion. "No," he had answered sadly, "real lions are big with furry manes. A cat could never look like that."

6

Daniel's parents had visited the animal shelter just a few days before to look for a pet to give Daniel on his birthday. The shelter had a lot of dogs, even more cats, three rabbits, two parrots, a turtle, an iguana and a miniature pig. They thought a dog would make the best pet for Daniel, but couldn't make up their mind about which one. They returned home to think about it.

Another day went by and Daniel kept talking about a lion for a pet. His parents did not know what to do until, suddenly, they thought of Charles. They remembered that he was big and very scruffy. His fur was so long all over his body you could barely see his friendly eyes, or his black nose, or floppy ears, or even much of his long tail. He just looked like a big hairy beast. Then they had the most wonderful idea: Daniel might get his lion after all.

So they returned to the shelter to get Charles. When he saw them coming Charles jumped up and greeted them with his furry tail wagging. He hoped they were coming to get him. And indeed they were.

Certificate of Adoption
"Charles"

9

After they left the shelter Daniel's parents took the dog straight to the pet groomer for a haircut. They told her exactly how they wanted the dog trimmed. The hair on the back of its body, on its underside, and on all four legs should be cut very short. On the dog's front it should be kept very long over the shoulders, chest, and neck and top of head. But its face should be trimmed short, as should the entire length of its tail except for the very end where she should leave a round tuft of long hair. Then when she was done trimming she should dye all of the long hair on the front of the dog and the tip of its tail a darker brown color to contrast with the short trimmed blond hair.

The groomer looked at Daniel's parents as if they were crazy, and then suddenly started laughing when she realized what they had in mind. This was going to be a lot of fun she thought, and got out her scissors. Charles did not know what was happening but thought he looked magnificent with his new haircut. He was happy to be going to a new home.

How to trim:

DYE

A LION DOG

You can just imagine Daniel's surprise and delight when on his special morning Daniel's parents covered his eyes and led him into the backyard to present him with a gift. "Happy birthday Daniel," they exclaimed.

Daniel opened his eyes and gasped; there in the backyard was an animal that certainly looked just like a lion. But instead of being scary it began jumping around wanting to play. "His name is Charles," said his mother. "And we hope he is enough of a lion for you."

Daniel knew immediately that this friendly animal could be his lion. "Thank you, thank you," he shouted and ran over to Charles. He put his arms around the big dog with the crazy haircut and hugged it for several minutes. He got a big, wet, sloppy kiss in return.

Daniel's mother explained: "One of his parents was a Labrador retriever and the other one was a poodle," she said. So that makes Charles a labradoodle." But to Daniel, Charles was all lion, and the best birthday gift ever.

12

Daniel and Charles quickly became the very best of friends. Daniel's parents thought it would be important to keep Charles at home until he became familiar with his surroundings, so the family's backyard became their playground. Every day they wrestled, played fetch and acted out really fun make-believe games.

One of their favorites was pretending Charles was a circus lion. Daniel would put a red vest on the dog and put him on a stool. He would then strut around snapping his homemade whip and Charles would bark and snarl and growl like a lion until Daniel ordered him down. Then both of them would run around the yard two times and bow to a pretend audience. Another favorite game was Wild Africa. Daniel pretended to be a game ranger on the lookout for lions. He put on khaki clothes and his jungle hat and hung binoculars around his neck. He carried his old wooden toy gun to protect himself against danger in the African bush. Daniel would search through the yard until he found Charles, hiding as a savage beast!

One weekend Daniel asked his parents if he could take Charles to the school playground just a block away. Since it was a quiet Saturday, Daniel's parents said yes. "Keep a close eye on Charles," they instructed Daniel. "He's not used to being away from home."

Daniel went on the swings and the slides and the hanging bars and climbed to the high fort. He called for Charles to come up with him. Charles tried but his paws were not made for climbing ladders. Daniel tried to help him up, but when he bent down Daniel lost his balance and fell. It was a bad fall and Daniel landed on his arm. It hurt a lot and he felt so sick he could not walk.

"Go get help," he told Charles and somehow, Charles understood. Charles ran back to the house and started barking. Daniel's mother and father followed the dog back to the playground where they found Daniel on the ground holding his arm and crying. Daniel's father tied a large handkerchief around Daniel's injury and carried him home. Then, straight to the hospital they went!

17

The doctor in the Emergency Room set Daniel's arm and wrapped it in a heavy cast. He told Daniel's parents that it was a bad break and he wanted to keep Daniel overnight for observation. Daniel was not pleased about having to spend the night alone in the hospital and his mother tried to comfort him. Back home Charles was restless. He would search around the house and yard for Daniel, whining frequently. Finally, that evening Daniel's father took Charles to the hospital during the visiting hours. Charles behaved very well so the nurse said he could go to Daniel's room. As soon as he saw Daniel his tail started wagging so fast that it looked like a propeller. He sat down next to the hospital bed and put his head on it up close to Daniel's head. Daniel reached over with his good arm and patted Charles and told him again what a good lion he was.

The other children in the hospital also loved Charles. Daniel's roommate Marcus said he even felt better when the friendly lion dog arrived. This made everybody laugh.

Daniel's arm healed quickly and soon the summer ended. It was time for school to begin. Daniel's mother let Charles walk to the bus stop at the corner with Daniel every morning and would send the loyal dog out again to meet Daniel there on his return every afternoon. Charles was a good pet and never wandered, but he hated being apart from Daniel. Then one day he decided to follow the school bus to see if he could join his best friend at school.

The bus drove faster than Charles could keep up, and soon he found himself lost in a neighborhood he didn't recognize. He smelled strange odors and saw a large area without houses. It had a sign that read Virginia Zoological Park. People he'd never seen before, and who certainly had never seen him either, started backing away from him and began calling quickly on their cell phones. It seemed very unfriendly to Charles and he suddenly felt frightened. He hid in some bushes the way he did when Daniel played Wild Africa with him.

From his hiding place Charles could hear people talking in loud, concerned voices. "There is a lion loose!" a man yelled into his cellphone when the 911 operator answered his call. "What?" the operator said. "Please repeat that sir." So he did. "There is a lion loose, I'm not kidding." The operator thought the man really sounded frightened, so she asked quickly. "Where did you see it?" "It's near the entrance to the zoo" he replied. Charles could hear more people making emergency 911 calls. "Is this 911?" screamed a frightened woman's voice. "I just saw a baby lion on Granby Street." Another man stammered, "Hello, 911? . . . I, I, I think a lion has escaped from the zoo."

Now Charles was really concerned. He remembered Daniel saying how large lions were. A big male could weigh up to 600 pounds! Charles knew that he only weighed 100 pounds. So he crouched farther down hoping that the escaped lion wouldn't find him hiding in the bushes.

22

The 911 operators had heard enough and they sent police and emergency vehicles to the scene. They called the mayor's office to alert them of the situation, then the zoo to ask if one of their male lions had escaped. The mayor was alarmed. He asked an operator if this could be a joke. She said, "No – the callers were all serious and people were running to get into their cars when they saw it."

When he got the message the director of the zoo called the curator and the curator called the big cat manager and the cat manager called the lion trainer. The trainer counted his lions and then he counted them again, starting from the other end of the line. All the lions were accounted for so the trainer told the manager "all of our lions are here." Then the manager called the curator and the curator called the director and the director called the 911 operator. Then everyone breathed a big sigh of relief. It wasn't one of the zoo's lions. But what lion had everyone seen? Was there an unknown beast on the prowl?

The police arrived first. They lined up their cars to form a barrier and then huddled with their chief for instructions. They had brought dart guns and big nets. Two of the officers had put on bulky animal attack suits. Just as they started to spread out to search for the lion out it walked from beneath some bushes.

While he had been hiding in the bushes Charles never saw a loose lion, or smelled it or even heard it. He also noticed that none of the birds or squirrels around him were worried. So after watching all the police commotion, he decided he would rather be with people than alone in the bushes if a real lion was on the loose.

As Charles walked toward the policemen the officers jumped to attention, began yelling and aimed their dart guns – at him! Then the police chief called out "Wait a minute!" He looked closely at Charles, rubbed his eyes and looked again. Suddenly he began to laugh. "That's not a lion," he exclaimed. "It's a dog! Although I can certainly see how someone might think otherwise."

26

That afternoon, after figuring out from his dog tags where Charles lived, the Chief of Police returned the wayward pet to its rightful owner. By then Daniel, who had just returned from school alone, had heard the story about an escaped lion from his excited mother, who had heard it on the television news. Daniel guessed what had happened. So when he saw Charles he exclaimed, "Where have you been? You scared all these people and we have been worried about you." Charles just wagged his tail faster. Daniel's mother apologized to the police and news people who were now on the front lawn. Everyone was laughing and joking about what they called the "Lion Dog."

Within a few days the story of Charles appeared in newspapers and on television stations around the world. Daniel and his pet were invited to appear on CNN and Good Morning America in New York. Videos of Charles on YouTube soon had over a million-and-a-half views. Charles even had his own Facebook page with more than 56,000 likes! The world was in love with Charles.

Then a wonderful thing happened right there in Daniel's and Charles' hometown. The athletic teams of a big university were all called the "Monarchs." The lion was their symbol. When people there heard about Charles they invited him to come to a basketball game. He did, and a student made up to look like a happy, large-headed lion took Charles onto the floor so the crowd could see him. Everybody cheered.

After people saw Charles at the basketball game, and heard all about his fame, they thought he would make a great mascot for the university. Daniel knew that other schools had dog mascots – why not a dog that looked like a lion as a lion mascot? At first he thought it was a great idea, but then he became concerned about Charles travelling all the time with the teams, and he knew he would miss him too much. Daniel said he would be happy to have Charles come to some home games when they wanted him, but he would prefer not to have him be the official, full-time mascot.

So Charles was invited many times. When it was a football game he, and the student dressed as the lion mascot, would run onto the field with the football team until they reached the opposite goal post. There the student would attach Charles' leash and lead him back while the band played a loud marching song. Charles would strut to the music. It was almost as if the mascot had a mascot. After the game he would wait outside for people to pet him and talk to him. He had become very popular and everybody loved the Lion Dog. Someone said "Charles has shown us that there is a little bit of lion in everyone."

As Charles grew bigger and his mane got longer he looked more and more like a lion. But he always knew that he was a dog. If dogs can laugh, it isn't hard to believe that he might be smiling to himself and thinking, "things are not always what they seem to be."